For Adam
R. H.

For Richard, my father
A. D.

First U.S. edition 2014

Library of Congress Catalog Card Number 2013955698
ISBN 978-0-7636-6517-3

14 15 16 17 18 19 SCP 10 9 8 7 6 5 4 3 2

Printed in Humen, Dongguan, China

This book was typeset in Quercus Hard.
The illustrations were done in watercolor.

Candlewick Press
99 Dover Street
Somerville, Massachusetts 02144

visit us at www.candlewick.com

Jim's LION

RUSSELL HOBAN
illustrated by
Alexis Deacon

CANDLEWICK PRESS

From his hospital bed

Jim was watching the snow whirling out of

the gray sky. He was looking sad. Nurse Bami

brought him hot chocolate. She was from

Africa; she had tribal scars on her cheeks.

She had seen lions, elephants, crocodiles.

"What's the matter?" said Bami.

"You know," said Jim.

"Tell me," said Bami. "Say it out."

"People who have what I have, mostly they die, don't they?" said Jim.

"Maybe the doctors can fix you up," said Bami.

"I've seen what they do on TV," said Jim. "They put you on a table and they put you to sleep and then they do the rest of it."

"Does that scare you?" said Bami.

"Yes," said Jim. "When I'm asleep I go to different places in my dreams but I always find my way back. I'm afraid that if the doctors put me to sleep they might send me somewhere that I can't get back from."

"Well, of course someone has to come looking for you," said Bami.

"Who can do that?" said Jim.

"Drink your hot chocolate," said Bami, "and I'll tell you.

"When you think of something, you see it in your head, don't you?"

"Sure I do," said Jim.

"Listen carefully now," said Bami. "This is not kid stuff."

"Good," said Jim.

"You've got all kinds of things in your head," said Bami, "everything you've ever seen or thought about, all in your head."

"I can't remember it all," said Jim.

"But it's all there," said Bami, "and there are all kinds of animals in there along with everything else."

"I guess there are," said Jim.

"One of those animals is the finder who can bring you back from wherever the doctors send you," said Bami.

"Which one?" said Jim.

"That's not for me to say," said Bami. "You must find your finder by yourself."

"How can I do that?" said Jim.

"That's what I'm going to tell you," said Bami.

"Close your eyes and let everything go away so your mind is empty."

Jim did that.

"Now," said Bami, "let a place come into your mind, a place where you really felt good. Don't tell me what it is; just let it come to you."

The place that came to Jim was a lonely

place by the sea. It was near an empty harbor that used to be full of fishing boats. He'd been there with Mom and Dad a long time ago, before his illness.

"When you see that place," said Bami, "let yourself hear it and smell it and taste it and touch it."

Jim did that. He saw the sea and the long, long sky in the summer afternoon. There was a great brown rock that stuck out of the sea; it was called the Lion's Head. Jim saw sandpipers flying low over the water; he heard the wind and the cries of the gulls. He heard the sighing of the sea and the hissing of it on the sand. He heard the pebbles clicking in the tide wash.

Jim smelled the salt wind and the sea and the sun-warm rocks on the beach. He put his hand in the water, felt the deep coldness of it and tasted the salt on his hand. He touched the rocks and felt the long years in them. He felt good in that place by the sea.

"Are you feeling good?" said Bami.

Jim didn't answer. He was smiling and he was asleep. He was in that good place by the sea.

He could feel

that he was waiting

for the moon to rise.

When it came up he saw that it was a full moon. The wet sand was all silvery with it. "Here I am," said Jim, "waiting." Then he saw a small dark shape far down the beach. Slowly it got bigger as it moved toward him.

It was a lion.

and woke up.

"Good morning,"

said Bami. "Don't tell me your dream; keep it inside you. Here comes breakfast."

"Why can't I tell you my dream?" said Jim.

"If it happened in your good place it might be a finding dream," said Bami, "and if you talk about it something goes out of it."

"Have you got a finder?" said Jim.

"Oh, yes," said Bami, "I'd have been dead three or four times already if my finder hadn't come looking for me."

"Is your finder an animal?" said Jim.

"Yes, but I won't say which one," said Bami.

"How did you find it?" said Jim.

"I went to my good place in a dream," said Bami, "and it came to me there."

"Did it, you know, scare you at all?" said Jim.

"Yes," said Bami. "That's how I knew it was the real thing. The real thing is always more than you're ready for. Of course I had my don't-run stone with me."

"A don't-run stone!" said Jim. "I haven't got one."

"Now you do," said Bami. She took a little painted pebble out of her pocket and gave it to Jim.

"Don't ask me any more

questions," she said.

"You must go on alone

from here."

TAP-TAP-TAP-TAP

APPETYTAPPETY
TAPTAPTAPPETTA
APPETYTAPTAPE
APTAPTAPTAPPETY
APPETYTAPTAP
TAPTAPTAPPETYL
TAP

crunch

NEXT

NEXT

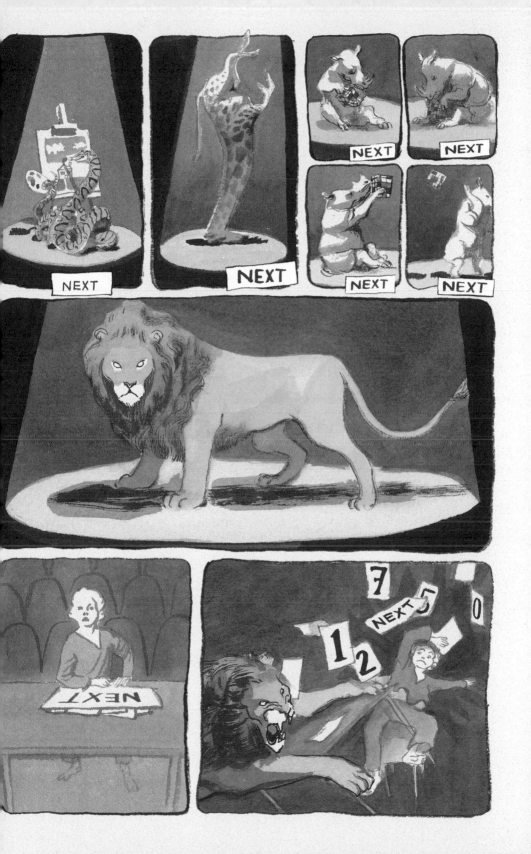

Jim's mom and dad

were talking to Jim's doctor, Dr. Monjo.

"Will Jim get better?" said Mom.

"It depends," said Dr. Monjo, "on what Jim has going for him."

"Don't you know?" said Mom. "Haven't you done all kinds of tests?"

"Yes," said Dr. Monjo, "but the tests don't always tell us why some people get better and others don't."

"Isn't there an operation you can do?" said Dad.

"There is," said Dr. Monjo, "but I'm not sure he's in good enough shape for it."

"When will you know?" said Dad.

"Let's see how he is in a day or two," said Dr. Monjo.

Mom and Dad brought Jim grapes and clementines and his big animal book that he'd asked for.

"Are you eating properly?" said Mom. "You have to keep your strength up."

"Yes," said Jim, "I'm eating properly and I'm feeling stronger all the time."

"That's the ticket," said Dad.

"Maybe you'll be home for Christmas," said Mom.

"I'm working on it," said Jim.

That night in his dream

Jim was back at the place by the sea. The moon was still full and the lion was still coming toward him.

Jim wanted to climb up the cliffs but he had the don't-run stone in his hand, so he didn't. "The real thing is always more than you're ready for," he said.

Closer and closer came the lion.

"Maybe," said Jim, "everything else was a dream and this is the only thing that's real."

Closer and closer came the lion. It opened its mouth and roared.

"Maybe this lion will eat me up," said Jim,

"and nobody will know that I didn't run."

Closer came the lion with its amber eyes,

its pink tongue, and its white teeth.

"Are you my finder?" said Jim.

The lion roared again.

ROAR

"Maybe that means yes," said Jim.

He stood where he was until the lion was

so close that he could smell its hot breath.

"I'm going to touch you," said Jim, "and

if you're my finder, you won't eat me up."

He stretched out his hand as the lion came

closer. Now the lion was right in front of Jim . . .

and he put his hand on its head . . .

and woke up.

"**Well, Jim,**" said Dr. Monjo, "the latest tests are looking pretty good and you're looking pretty good too."

"I feel good," said Jim. He was remembering how he'd put his hand on the lion's head.

"I'll have to talk to your mom and dad," said Dr. Monjo, "but first I want to talk to you. There's an operation that could help you but there's always some danger and I want you to tell me how you feel about it. Do you want to do it?"

"Yes," said Jim, "let's do it."

"You sound very confident," said Dr. Monjo.

"I know you're a good doctor," said Jim, "and the rest of it I'll leave to my finder."

"Who's your finder?" said Dr. Monjo.

"I mustn't say," said Jim.

When they came to wheel Jim into the operating room Bami kissed him and said, "Now's a good time for a quick visit to your good place just to check in with your finder."

"Right," said Jim. "I forgot to thank you

for the don't-run stone. I've got it in my hand now."

"You're welcome," said Bami. "Good luck, Jim. See you later."

"Thanks," said Jim. "See you."

Jim looked out at the gray sky and the snow on the roofs of the hospital buildings and the Christmas lights of the stores across the street. Then he closed his eyes and he was in his good place.

There was no moon but in the starlight he could see the lion sitting on the beach the way a dog sits. It was waiting for him.

Jim looked into the lion's amber eyes and the lion opened its mouth and roared.

"Okay," said Jim, "let's do it."

He walked down the long curve of the beach into the dark and the lion followed.

On Christmas morning

Jim came downstairs in his pajamas and looked at the Christmas tree with its twinkling lights. He remembered how his lion looked coming through the dark to find him.

"Merry Christmas!" said Mom and Dad.

"Merry Christmas," said Jim. "I haven't had a chance to get your presents."

"You're our present," said Mom.

"The best that could ever be," said Dad.

Jim got a train set and a computer game from Mom and Dad. There was another box, a small one. Jim opened it and there was a beach pebble inside the wrappings.

On it was written:

This is to remember me by.

It is from my good place.

Love XX, Bami.